Secret Forests

Secret Forests

By Michael Gaffney

AN ARTISTS & WRITERS GUILD BOOK
Golden Books
Western Publishing Company, Inc.

HOW TO USE THIS BOOK

Creepy crawly bugs and insects come in all different shapes and sizes. Some are brightly colored; some are the same color as their surroundings and are difficult to see. This blending into the background is called camouflage. *Secret Forests* will show you different kinds of bugs and insects in their natural habitat. As you turn the pages, you will see how very effective their camouflage is.

Look at each page of creepy crawlies and read the information about them. Then turn the page and look carefully at the full-page illustration for each habitat. How many camouflaged creatures can you spot?

CONTENTS

Tropical Forest

These bugs and insects all live in Southeast Asia, where the climate is hot and wet. The thick green bushes make an excellent home for many crawling and flying creatures.

Forester moth
During the day, this moth sleeps deep in the darkest shadows of a bush, safely hidden from prying eyes.

Jumping spider
This spider's big eyes help it to look out for danger and spot prey from far away. Its long jump means that it can catch its prey unaware.

Lanternfly
The head of this lanternfly is long and thin. It uses its mouth, which is shaped like a straw, to suck the sap from trees.

Praying mantis
This long, thin mantis hides so that it can pounce on its unsuspecting victims and take them by surprise.

Bush cricket

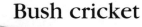

Leaf insect

The bush cricket and the leaf insect look like dead, dry leaves. Their protective coloration keeps them hidden from other animals.

Leaf beetles

Tough-skinned leaf beetles are difficult to crush. Other animals soon learn to avoid this well-protected insect.

Tortoise beetle

This beetle hides under leaves to remain safe from predators. Its body is so flat that it does not even cast a shadow.

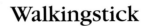

Walkingstick

Walkingsticks remain very still, looking like twigs. In this way, they avoid being eaten.

Cicada

Cicadas are so good at hiding that they sometimes have difficulty finding each other! Their loud song tells other cicadas where they are.

Jungle glory butterfly

This butterfly keeps a colorful secret. When it flaps its wings, the patches on them appear to flash brightly, and its enemies are too startled to attack.

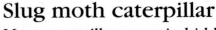

Slug moth caterpillar

Most caterpillars remain hidden from predators while they are eating. The slug moth caterpillar's spine makes it easy to blend in on a leaf and harder for other animals to eat.

9

TROPICAL FOREST FLOOR

The floor of the African tropical forest is dark and damp, a place of rotting vegetation. A multitude of creepy crawlies feed there on dead plants, tree roots—and each other.

Army ants
No insect survives a meeting with a marching mob of army ants. Larger soldier ants defend the workers, who kill and carry off any creature that gets in their way.

Giant millipede
This is the world's biggest millipede, as long as a man's forearm. It burrows through the soil like an armored tank.

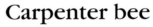

Carpenter bee
The male carpenter bee is very fierce and will attack any other insect that comes near its home. It makes its home in the rotting wood of trees or in the soil on the forest floor.

Hercules beetle
Male Hercules beetles use their huge horns to fight other males. The beetle's massive size protects it from insect predators, while its tough outside makes it impossible for larger hunters, such as birds, to attack.

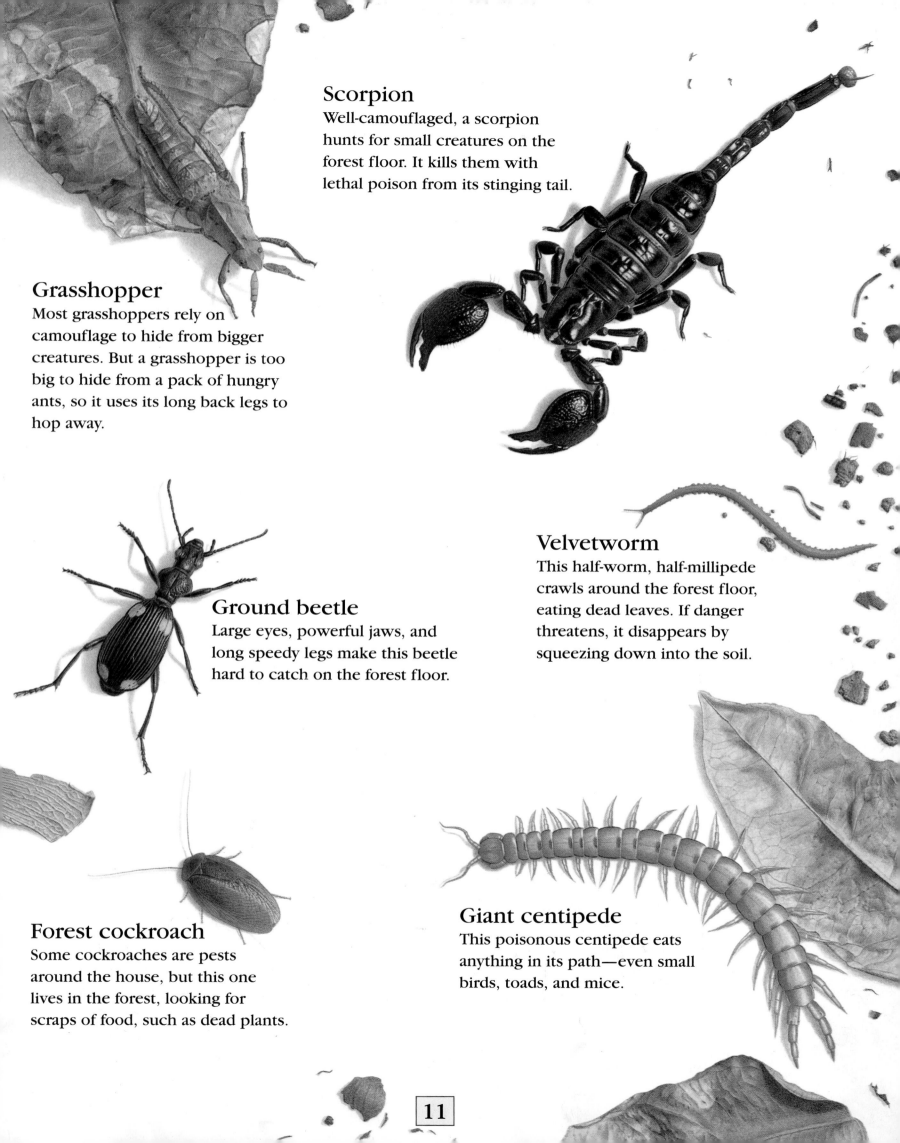

Scorpion

Well-camouflaged, a scorpion hunts for small creatures on the forest floor. It kills them with lethal poison from its stinging tail.

Grasshopper

Most grasshoppers rely on camouflage to hide from bigger creatures. But a grasshopper is too big to hide from a pack of hungry ants, so it uses its long back legs to hop away.

Ground beetle

Large eyes, powerful jaws, and long speedy legs make this beetle hard to catch on the forest floor.

Velvetworm

This half-worm, half-millipede crawls around the forest floor, eating dead leaves. If danger threatens, it disappears by squeezing down into the soil.

Forest cockroach

Some cockroaches are pests around the house, but this one lives in the forest, looking for scraps of food, such as dead plants.

Giant centipede

This poisonous centipede eats anything in its path—even small birds, toads, and mice.

OAK LEAVES

Oak trees grow in many countries around the world. Their juicy leaves are home to many winged insects. Some creatures, such as the carrion beetle and the orbweb spider, prey on insects that live near the oak leaves.

Carrion beetle
This beetle scavenges among the leaves, hunting for food. It feeds on the remains of dead animals.

Stinkbug
This bug uses its long, thin mouth to suck the juicy sap from plants. When in danger, it gives off a terrible odor, causing attackers to leave it alone.

Tortrix moth
Because of its color, the tortrix moth seems to disappear when it lands on a leaf. Its caterpillar hides inside rolled-up leaves or dangles from a silk thread if attacked.

Tree cricket
This cricket has long, powerful back legs to help it jump far away from danger. It lays its eggs in tree bark or in a dried-up gall left by a gall wasp, just like the one shown on the next page.

Purple hairstreak butterfly
This butterfly thrives high in the air. It flutters around the tops of oaks and rests on high leaves, licking up the sap spilled by other feeding insects.

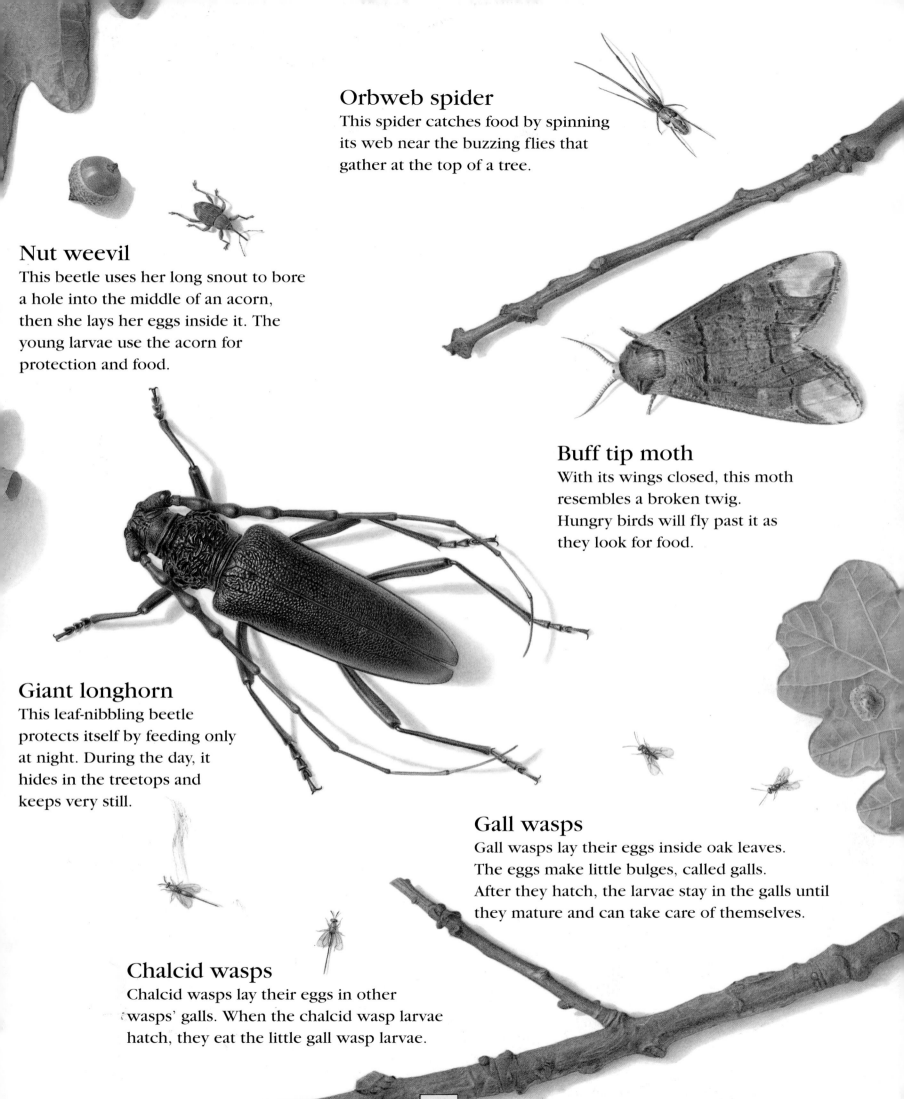

Orbweb spider

This spider catches food by spinning its web near the buzzing flies that gather at the top of a tree.

Nut weevil

This beetle uses her long snout to bore a hole into the middle of an acorn, then she lays her eggs inside it. The young larvae use the acorn for protection and food.

Buff tip moth

With its wings closed, this moth resembles a broken twig. Hungry birds will fly past it as they look for food.

Giant longhorn

This leaf-nibbling beetle protects itself by feeding only at night. During the day, it hides in the treetops and keeps very still.

Gall wasps

Gall wasps lay their eggs inside oak leaves. The eggs make little bulges, called galls. After they hatch, the larvae stay in the galls until they mature and can take care of themselves.

Chalcid wasps

Chalcid wasps lay their eggs in other wasps' galls. When the chalcid wasp larvae hatch, they eat the little gall wasp larvae.

Leaf Litter Creatures

In autumn many trees lose their leaves. This leaf litter and the dead wood nearby form a carpet on the ground. It is full of small creatures that find food and shelter in the fallen leaves.

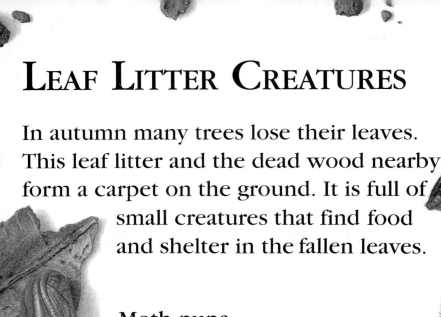

Moth pupa
Sealed in a protective case called a pupa, a caterpillar transforms into a moth. It is well hidden to avoid being eaten by other animals.

False scorpion
This tiny creature gets its name because it resembles a scorpion but does not have a poisonous tail. In fact, it has no stinger and lives hidden away in pieces of rotting wood.

Violet ground beetle
This beetle feeds on slugs. It chews them up with its strong jaws and sucks out their juicy insides.

Earwig
A mother earwig takes great care of her eggs. She lays them in soil, then stands constant guard, licking the eggs to keep them clean until they hatch.

Springtails
These silvery soil-dwellers have a special tail hidden under their bodies. Whenever danger threatens, this tail helps them spring to safety.

Netted slug
This slug looks like it has no protection, but when it is attacked it becomes very sticky. This discourages most of the animals that try to eat it—but not all of them!

Earthworm
Earthworms eat the soil and leaves on the woodland floor. As they munch away, they churn up the soil, making it easier for plants to grow.

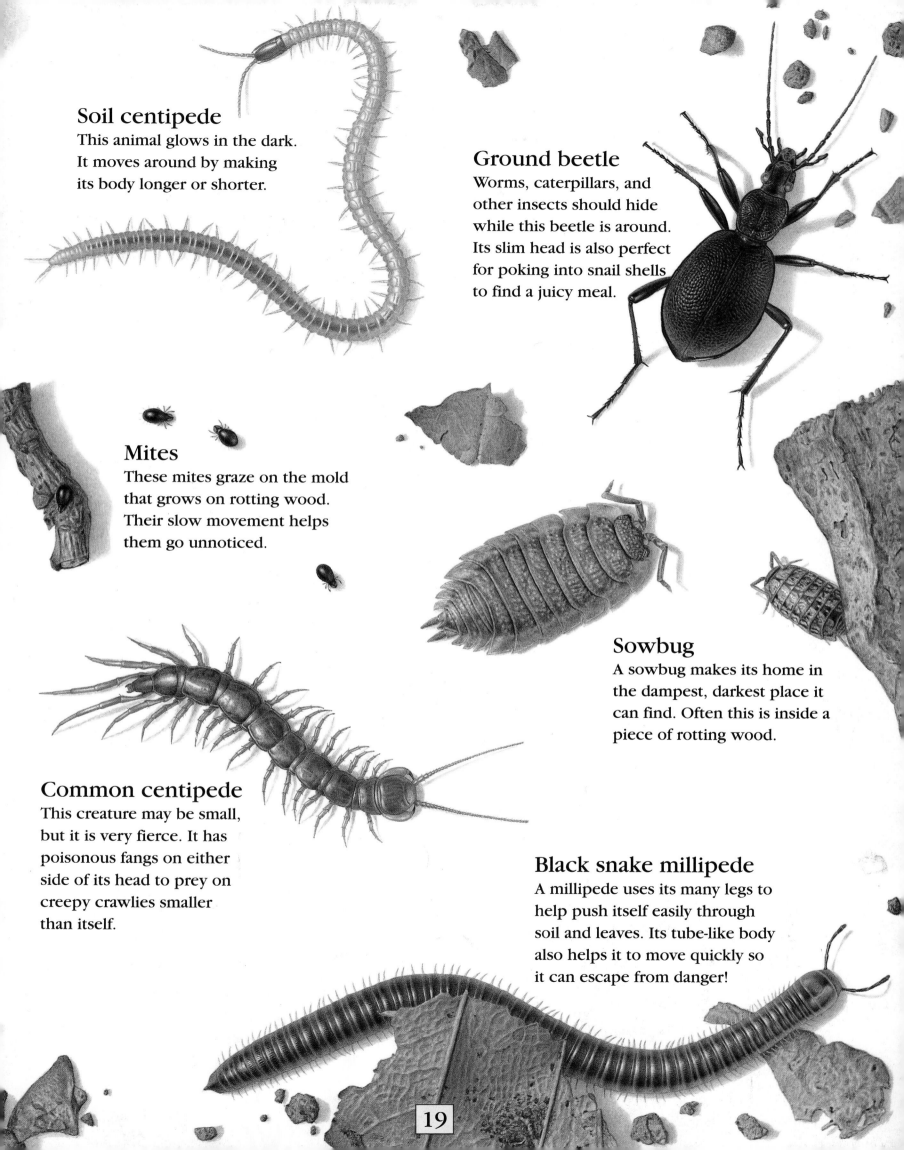

Soil centipede

This animal glows in the dark. It moves around by making its body longer or shorter.

Ground beetle

Worms, caterpillars, and other insects should hide while this beetle is around. Its slim head is also perfect for poking into snail shells to find a juicy meal.

Mites

These mites graze on the mold that grows on rotting wood. Their slow movement helps them go unnoticed.

Sowbug

A sowbug makes its home in the dampest, darkest place it can find. Often this is inside a piece of rotting wood.

Common centipede

This creature may be small, but it is very fierce. It has poisonous fangs on either side of its head to prey on creepy crawlies smaller than itself.

Black snake millipede

A millipede uses its many legs to help push itself easily through soil and leaves. Its tube-like body also helps it to move quickly so it can escape from danger!

Pine Forest Bark

In cooler countries, pine trees, with their needle-like leaves and cones, grow in thick forests. Very few insects living there adapt to the cold, dark, dry pine forest floor. Most of the insects live on—or underneath—the tree bark.

Pine ladybug

Pine ladybugs are usually found on pine needles. Their spots indicate to would-be predators that they taste awful.

Barklice

The tiny size of barklice makes them difficult to see. They will eat anything —even bark!

Horntail

A female horntail burrows into a tree trunk with her long, thin tail to lay her eggs. Her wood-eating horntail larvae hatch out under the bark of the tree. Few predators can reach them there.

Ichneumon wasp

Tree bark doesn't save horntail larvae from the ichneumon wasp. The female ichneumon pokes her long tail through the bark and lays eggs inside the horntail larvae! When the eggs hatch, the larvae eat the horntail alive.

Sap beetle

The small dark-colored sap-beetle is well hidden in the forest. It lives on the sticky sap that oozes from a tree when its bark gets damaged.

Eyed ladybug

This ladybug spends its whole life on pine trees. It crawls over the branches, looking for other insects to eat.

Snakefly

The snakefly's long neck helps it look over the bumps on tree bark, trying to spot other creatures hiding there.

Combfooted spider

A bark crevice is normally a safe place for a small insect to hide, but not if this spider is lurking inside.

Pine beauty moth

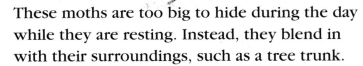

Pine hawk moth

These moths are too big to hide during the day while they are resting. Instead, they blend in with their surroundings, such as a tree trunk.

Spruce bark beetles

The larvae of this beetle live under tree bark, spreading disease. The larvae grow under the bark until they become adults and then bore holes so they can escape.

Clerid beetle

The clerid beetle eats harmful bark beetles, hunting for them along cracks in the tree. In this way, it saves trees from other insects.

25

PINE FOREST FLOOR

The few insects that do live on the pine forest floor crawl among the fallen pine needles and cones. They look for seeds, dead wood, or other insects to eat.

Robber fly
This fierce-looking fly jumps out from the bushes like a ruthless robber, sometimes preying on insects larger than itself.

Timberman
Predators don't spot this beetle because it blends in well with its surroundings. This timberman is sitting still, hidden from everything— except a mate.

Pine weevil
After it has spent the summer feeding on bark in the trees, this beetle searches the ground for a safe place to sleep through the winter.

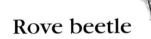

Rove beetle
You might spot a rove beetle near a dead animal. He will probably be hunting for maggots that have hatched from eggs laid by flies.

False blister beetle
This beetle spends all its young life inside plants and fallen branches. It feeds on them, safely away from birds and mice.

Greenbottle

A feeding greenbottle first spits on its food to make liquid. It then laps this up with its sponge-like tongue.

Seed bug

A seed bug tucks itself safely inside a pine cone to eat the seeds.

Sexton beetle

Have you ever wondered what happens to small mammals and birds when they die? Some of them are used by this beetle. She lays her eggs on the remains of the dead animal, so when her young hatch they have a ready-made food supply.

Money spiders

These spiders spin their webs across dark holes on the woodland floor. Animals looking for a safe place to hide are trapped in the web for the spider's next meal.

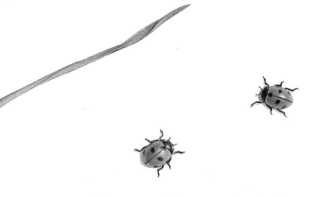

Scarce 7-spot ladybug

This is the only ladybug that can safely live near the nests of wood ants, which will attack other kinds of ladybugs.

Wood ant

Packs of wood ants aren't frightened of anything because the have a secret weapon—they can spray their victim with acid.

CREATURE INDEX

A page number in *italics* indicates an illustration only.

For Phillip and Katie
M.G.

The text has been checked for accuracy by
Dr. Norman Platnick, Curator, Department of Entomology,
American Museum of Natural History, New York City.

ISBN: 0-307-17505-7
Printed in Singapore.   A MCMXCIV

First published by David Bennett Books, St. Albans, England.

Library of Congress Cataloging-in-Publication Data

Gaffney, Michael, 1967-
Secret forests/by Michael Gaffney
p.   cm.

1. Forest insects—Juvenile literature. 2. Arthropoda—Juvenile literature.
3. Forest fauna—Habitat—Juvenile literature. [1. Insects. 2. Arthropods.
3. Forest animals.] I. Title.
QL467.2.G34   1994
595.70909'52—dc20   93-36275   CIP   AC

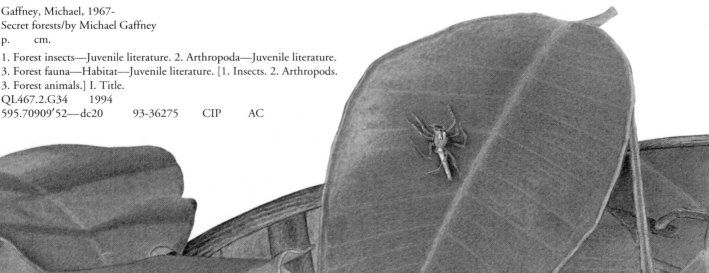

Ground spider

Take another look. Did you see
this spider? It manages to keep hidden
in the leaf litter on the forest floor.
The female of this species kills the
male after mating.